HOLIDAY FOR A HERO

A SWEET HEROES AT HEART COMPANION
NOVELLA

MARYANN JORDAN

Holiday for a Hero(Heroes at Heart) Copyright 2020

Cover Design by: Designs by Stacy

ISBN ebook: 978-1-947214-76-7

ISBN print: 978-1-947214-77-4

❀ Created with Vellum

DEDICATION

As a adolescent counselor for over twenty-five years, I had the opportunity to work with many young people. One young man, upset over a poor choice he had made, came to me. As I listened to his story and his confession, I told him that the true measure of a man was not in the mistakes he made, but in how he handled those mistakes. I remember the look on his face when I told him I was sure he was going to be a good man.

So this book is dedicated to all the students over the years who allowed me to be a part of their lives.

FOREWORD

There are times in an author's life when an idea is born... a subtle memory whispered into our ear that blossoms into a novel, or perhaps, even a series.

If you read the dedication to this book, you will know where the idea came from. But, what I could not imagine was the impact this series had on readers.

Many have told me that Miss Ethel is the most beloved character they have ever encountered in any book... something that is humbling, and yet, understandable.

She is patterned after many women I know, especially my mother.

Readers wanted her story and so I am proud to offer to you the background of Miss Ethel in this sweet, companion novella.

I hope you enjoy... I know I have enjoyed creating her.

Maryann Jordan

Ethel Morgenstern stood on one side of the room with her girlfriends. The others were giggling and chatting, but Ethel observed the room around her. The church reception hall was gaily lit with Christmas greenery, red and gold ribbons, and candles nestled amongst the punch bowls and food on the long table.

Her friends looked toward the teenage boys standing on the opposite side of the room and speculated on who they hoped would ask them to dance. Tall and slender, as tall as some of the boys around, Ethel lacked the pronounced curves of some of the other girls. Assuming she wouldn't be asked to dance, she spent her time casting her gaze toward the middle of the floor where numerous couples were already dancing under the watchful eye of the chaperones. A grin slipped past her calm demeanor at the sight of the adults determined to supervise the dancing so there would always be a space between the couple.

A few of the girls' dresses were shorter than hers,

and she sighed as she smoothed her hands over her skirt. Her mother might have acquiesced a little on the length of her skirt, but her father would never give into shorter styles. Her dark hair hung in thick waves over her shoulders, but again, she looked toward the other girls with envy. Most of their permed hair was teased into bouffants.

"Ethel!"

Snapping her head around, she blushed. "I'm sorry, what did you say?"

The giggling ensued once again, and her best friend, Jennifer, asked, "Who do you have your eye on?"

Pushing her glasses slightly up on her nose, she shrugged. Horn rimmed glasses with the little fake jewel in the upper corners might've been fashionable, but she knew it made her look more intellectual than attractive. Even her name was not cute. *Ethel.* It sounded so old-fashioned. Shoving that thought to the side, she replied, "No one special. I'm just glad we all turned sixteen years old before the holidays." For several years, the church had been offering a well-chaperoned holiday party for teenagers. She and Jennifer had counted down the months until they'd be able to attend.

As her friends slowly drifted away, accepting dances from some of the young men, she swayed to the music, lost in her own thoughts.

The idea of Elizabeth and Jane Bennet from Pride and Prejudice ran through her mind, and her lips curved into a grin once more. It struck her that even though the story took place in a previous century, the tale was little changed. Young men and young women hoping to pair together at a dance.

As her gaze continued to drift over the other teens in the room, she blinked as her attention was captured by the dark eyes of the most handsome young man she'd ever seen. Tall and strapping, his dark hair combed over, slightly longer than she knew her mother would have liked. But it only served to make Ethel want to reach out and smooth it back from his forehead. Her feet stayed rooted to the floor, unable to move away from the newcomer's steady gaze. Her breath caught in her throat when she realized he was walking toward her.

He wore a white shirt, the sleeves rolled up over his forearms, a blue tie, and navy pants. Appropriate, and yet casual. It was easy to see why the other girls in the room halted what they were doing just to stare, and she had no doubt they hoped he would stare at them. But for some inexplicable reason, his gaze never left hers. She fought the urge to reach up and fiddle with her glasses again but instead tucked a long dark tress of hair behind her ear. Before she knew it, he was standing directly in front of her. Much to her surprise, she had to lean her head back to look into his face. She jerked when his fingers touched hers.

Looking down, he gently took her hand and pulled her forward to the dance floor. With one hand placed on her lower back and his other hand clutching hers between them, they swayed to the music. He remained quiet, and she didn't speak for fear of breaking the spell and finding that she was actually standing by herself in the middle of the floor with nothing but a foolish, dreamy expression on her face. But his fingers flexed, and she felt his fiery brand on her back. She leaned slightly away, peered upward into his dark eyes, and was lost. Lost and found, all in the same instant.

"What were you smiling about before I came over?"

His voice was deep and soothing and held none of the squeak of the young teenage boys, causing her to wonder how old he was. Blushing, she knew if she told him the truth, he would find her ridiculous. But for the life of her, she couldn't think of anything clever to say. "I was thinking of Pride and Prejudice..." Expecting him to drop her hand, laugh in her face, and turn away, she was stunned when he pulled her tighter.

"Dare I hope that you would be Elizabeth Bennett to my Mr. Darcy?"

She blinked at his recognition of the Jane Austen story as her breath caught in her throat and no words came forth.

"You are too generous to trifle with me."

She continued to stare as he quoted from the book, and she shook her head. "Please, don't tease me."

His eyes narrowed slightly as he asked, "What's your name?"

She swallowed deeply. "Ethel."

"I'm George. George Wiseman. And Miss Ethel, I think you're the most beautiful girl I've ever seen. I would never tease you."

He pulled her back tightly, and the air left her lungs as she remained in his embrace. The evening passed, and she stayed in his arms, separating only when the chaperones eyed them with suspicion. As the last hour of the dance wound down, he stopped and looked up at the mistletoe hanging above them. With every fiber of her being, she wanted him to kiss her but felt certain that her first kiss would not be at the church social. Like everything so far with George, he surprised her. As she stared into his dark eyes lit by the twinkling candlelight, he lifted his hand and cupped her jaw, kissing her lightly.

"Miss Ethel," he whispered, "I think it's only fair to warn you."

Her heart beat wildly in her chest, horrified by what his warning might be.

He shocked her when he said, "You're the girl I'm going to marry." With that, he kissed her lightly again.

Six Years Later

"Are your eyes still shut?"

Ethel Wiseman giggled and turned her head toward her husband. She lifted her hand and patted the scarf tied around her eyes. "George, how on earth do you think I can see anything with his blindfold on?" She heard his chuckle and added, "Although, why the need for such mystery, I don't understand."

"I wanted to do something special for our second anniversary," he replied.

The sentiment was nice but hardly gave her an explanation. The breeze through the open car window captured her long dark hair, and she hoped it would not become tangled. "If I'd known we were going for such a long drive, I would have worn a scarf around my hair."

"You're absolutely beautiful, Ethel. Messy hair or not."

Her eye roll was hidden by the blindfold, but before she had a chance to retort, she felt the car slowing. The sounds of children playing in the distance could be heard, and she could not imagine where George was taking her.

Two years. It was hard to imagine she'd been married for two years. She had wanted to be his wife ever since she first saw him, never forgetting their kiss and his declaration.

Her thoughts were jerked back to the present when the car came to a stop. She heard the gearshift move into park and the creak of the brake.

"Well, we're here," George announced.

"Well, since I don't know where *here* is, can I take my blindfold off now?"

"Absolutely not!"

Before she had a chance to speak, she heard his door open and the sounds of him climbing out, closing his door, and footsteps making their way around the car. Soon, her door was opened, and he held her hand, assisting her out of the vehicle.

He gently untied the knot at the back of her head, and she blinked in the December sunlight. Wrapping her coat tightly around her body, she snuggled closer as his arm draped over her shoulder. Glancing around, she spied a quaint neighborhood. Each house on the street was different, of various sizes, most with Christmas wreaths hanging on their doors. She twisted her head around to look at him, expecting an explanation.

"Come on," he said, not giving her a chance to question. He pulled her in tightly to his side, leading her past the white picket fence gate and up the sidewalk toward the house at the end of the cul-de-sac.

Her head leaned back as they approached, noting the large, white, two-story house with the wide front porch. A small copse of trees grew to one side, and it appeared that straw-covered flower beds were scattered about the yard. "Whose house is this?" she asked as he marched straight up the steps to the front door. Much to her surprise, he didn't ring the doorbell but instead pulled a key out of his pocket.

He quickly unlocked the door and threw it open, and before she had a chance to ask questions, he bent and scooped her up with one arm under her knee and the other securely supporting her back. Throwing her arms around his neck, she squealed. "George Wiseman! Have you lost your mind? What are you doing?"

He chuckled, and she felt the rumble throughout her body as he stepped over the threshold, kicked the door closed to keep out the cold, and placed her feet gently onto the floor.

Holding her gaze, he bent low. His eyes twinkled as he said, "Welcome home, Ethel."

Home? Dragging her gaze from his enthusiastic expression, she looked around, seeing a large living room void of all furniture except for a wingback chair near the fireplace, an easy chair opposite it, and a Christmas tree in the corner. The built-in bookshelves along one wall stood empty. There was no other furniture to be seen. Still in his arms, she looked at him, questions bombarding her from all sides. "I don't understand!"

"I've been saving, sweetheart. With the money I got from the Army and what I've been making down at the shop, I put every dime aside that I could. Yesterday when you thought I was out running errands, I put a down payment on this house. It's my present to you."

As his words sank in, she gasped, throwing her arms around his neck. Pulling her up against him, he began to twirl in a circle in the middle of the almost-empty living room.

"I know we've got furniture from our apartment to bring over, but I went ahead and bought that nice chair for you. Just thinking about seeing you sitting there reading or knitting or bouncing our children on your knee made me not wait before I bought it."

She opened and closed her mouth several times, the words not coming as she battled the overwhelming emotions. Finally, she managed to croak, "I can't believe you bought us a house!" He continued to twirl her around, and she laughed, throwing her arms out wide.

"Let me show it to you, darling."

He took the lead, and she trailed along with him as they looked at the bookcases, knowing that over the years they would fill them with the books that they loved to read and share. He led her into the dining room, and she was stunned at the size.

"Oh, my goodness! This will hold a huge table."

"I figured we'd need it with the brood we're going to have," he said, winking.

Blushing, she followed him down the hall to discover the massive kitchen. A washer and dryer were tucked into the utility room that led to the backyard. Braving the cold, she stepped onto the back patio and looked around at the wide, fenced backyard.

"I figured this yard would be big enough for our sons to play ball."

Twisting her head and looking up, she grinned. "We might have all girls, you know?"

He kissed her deeply, then whispered, "Whatever God blesses us with is what we'll love."

Hustling back inside, she spied the downstairs bedroom, complete with a small bathroom. Upstairs, she was shocked once more to discover two huge bedrooms and a large bathroom at the end of the hall. A smaller room, complete with a small bathroom, was attached.

"We can pick one of these big ones to be ours, and I figure the little one can be the nursery. As other kids come along, they can share one of the other big rooms."

"When can we move in?" she asked, bouncing on her toes with excitement.

"The shop is closed tomorrow, and I've got some of the fellows that are going to come to get all of our furniture out of our apartment. So, starting tomorrow night, we'll be here in our own bed."

Her smile spread widely, and she shook her head. "I can't believe you did this, George. I had no idea you were up to this."

"Don't you know, sweet girl, I'd do anything for you?"

They walked downstairs and settled next to the fireplace and the Christmas tree in their new, comfortable chairs. Talking long into the night, planning for the future, she couldn't imagine a better Christmas... other than thinking about the many Christmases they would share in their new home.

2

TEN YEARS LATER

The scent of sugar, vanilla, and cinnamon filled the house as Ethel bustled around the kitchen. With her hands resting on her hips, she stared at the counter filled with platters of Christmas cookies, quickly counting how many dozens she'd made and how many more she needed to finish.

The radio was blaring a channel offering holiday carols, all of which she knew by heart, proved as she sang along to the joyful tunes. The church was having its annual holiday party for the little children, hence the many cookies she was baking. A smile slipped across her face as she thought of the excited expressions on the children when they walked in and saw the tables loaded with goodies.

Just as quickly as her smile had come, it slid from her lips. Children. She and George had enjoyed practicing to make a baby, but each month, year after year, brought disappointment. She had gone to her doctor, continually assured that *'it will happen when it happens'*.

She had visited the library, reading every book and medical journal she could lay her hands on about getting pregnant. George had assured her over and over that as much as he would love to have children with her, she was the joy in his life. *But I want to give him children.* She had prayed, spending hours on her knees with her hands clasped, making promises and vows if only she could have a child.

Hearing the front door open, she shoved those thoughts away and quickly wiped her hands on her apron. She hurried past the dining room with its large table covered in a bright red cloth and Christmas greenery decorating the middle, her smile firmly on her face again.

George stood in the foyer, stamping his feet and rubbing his hands together. "It's as cold as can be out there, Ethel girl. Sure does feels warm in here and smells good!"

She walked straight up to him, lifted on her toes, and met his lips for a kiss. She could not remember a day that he had come home and they hadn't greeted each other the same way. "Come on in, and I'll get you a cup of coffee. Do you want to have it in the living room?"

A small fire was already lit, and with the decorated tree in the corner of the room, the space was inviting. Instead of taking her offer, he lifted his head and sniffed loudly. Laughing, she said, "I get the feeling that you'd like a cookie, as well."

"Absolutely. And don't worry about serving me in here, I'll just have my coffee and cookies in the kitchen with you. I know you're busy."

They walked down the hall together, and George sat on a stool at the kitchen counter while she poured him a cup of coffee. Strong, with just a dash of cream.

He took a sip, smiled, and nodded. "You make the best coffee, Ethel." His gaze landed on the platters of cookies directly in front of him, and his smile widened. "You also make the best cookies!"

Pleased with his compliment, she grabbed a small plate and placed three cookies on top. "Well, for such a sweet talker, I think you should have a reward."

He reached out and snagged a snickerdoodle. As he munched the warm cookie, a blissful expression crossed his face. Turning back to her mixing bowl, she continued to stir the next batch of batter when she heard him sigh heavily.

"Is everything okay?" When he didn't answer right away, she twisted her head, spying his furrowed brow.

"Would you mind making some extra cookies?"

"Of course not. Did you want to take some to work? I was going to make extra for you anyway."

He shook his head slowly. "No, no, not for work. I thought we might take some to one of the shelters."

His request surprised her, not certain she understood what he was referring to. "Shelters?"

He was quiet for a moment, so she laid the spoon in the bowl and turned so she could give him her full attention. Leaning her hip against the counter, she could see thoughts working behind his eyes and remained quiet, knowing he would speak when he was ready.

His shoulders hefted as he sighed heavily again.

"Had someone come in today, and I could tell they were down on their luck. I offered them some coffee, even though it was the office version and not your good brew."

She smiled at the compliment, then continued to wait for the rest of his story.

"The man needed some work on his car to get to a new job. He, his wife, and two boys were living in a shelter down on Canter Street. I asked him a few questions and found out it was a shelter for people that had lost their homes and didn't have any other place to go."

Ethel worried her bottom lip as she watched George visibly struggle with his story. She read the newspaper and listened to the news each night, considering herself to be well versed in the woes of the world. She understood the plight of people who needed assistance, but somehow, they'd always seemed far off, and it felt as though the work she did at her church was enough. Staring at George, concern knitted his brow and the worry for this family deepened the creases radiating from his eyes.

She reached out and placed her hand on his, squeezing lightly. Of course, I'll make more cookies," she said, embarrassed at the grateful look he shot her. "I should have thought of something like this myself."

Shaking his head, he said, "Don't take that on, Ethel. You do a lot for the neighbors, community, and church. I sure as heck don't want to add more onto you—"

Waving her other hand dismissively, she replied, "Oh posh, George. Making a few more cookies is hardly piling any work onto me."

He held her gaze and smiled, the love tangible between them. "I'm going to go get cleaned up, and then I can help you take these to the church. I'll take the extra tomorrow and drop them off at the shelter."

"You'll do no such thing," she declared. "We'll take them to the shelter together."

Bundled against the cold, Ethel and George walked into the shelter. Her glove-covered hands were loaded with plastic containers of cookies. Uncertain what she would face, she took her cue from George's quiet strength. As they walked in, he moved to the reception desk, explaining why they were there. Ethel's gaze scanned the worn but clean tile floor and the large bulletin board on the wall, covered in notes for the residents.

"Mr. Wiseman?"

Hearing his name, she and George turned in unison, spying a thin man, his hair swept back from his face. Leaving her side, George walked over and stuck out his hand. "Jonathan," he greeted. "Call me George." He turned and lifted his arm and Ethel hurried over. "This is my wife, Ethel."

"We brought some cookies for the children here. George thought your kids might like some."

Jonathan ducked his head, but she could see gratitude filling his being. His gratitude settled awkwardly on her shoulders... she had so much and he so little. Just then, a small woman with two boys in tow made their way into the lobby. The woman's eyes were large but wary. As her husband introduced his wife, Sue, she offered a little smile as her gaze darted toward Ethel. Once the introductions were over, George maneuvered the gathering toward the corner of the room where there were a small sofa and several chairs.

The boys were shy, hanging behind their mother. Ethel knelt so that she was on their level, popped the top off the plastic container, and held out the treats. "Would you like some cookies?"

They both looked up at their mother, who offered a quick nod. "Get just one and mind your manners."

The boys dutifully stepped forward and each took one cookie, offering their thanks before darting back toward their mother. Ethel wanted to offer them more, but it dawned on her that filling up on sweets might not be what their mother wanted.

They settled in their seats, George making small talk with Jonathan, finding out how his job interview went. The relief in their faces was evident when he said that he'd be starting the next week and hoped to move his family out of the shelter and into a small apartment soon after. Her attention was drawn to the two boys. She smiled and lifted a brow at their mother, who met her unasked question with a nod. Pushing the plastic container toward them again, she whispered, "Please, have another cookie. And then, if there are other children in the shelter you'd like to share them with, that would be lovely."

The boys grew bolder, and soon they were chatting with her, warming her heart with their stories. Wanting babies of her own did not keep her from enjoying the company of other children.

As they stood to leave, Sue accepted Ethel's hug and whispered softly, "Thank you so much."

"Charles Dickens once said, *'No one is useless in this world who lightens the burdens of another.'*" Seeing the boys' wide eyes, she explained, "That was from a book I enjoyed reading. I like to memorize quotes."

"We don't have any books. We have to leave them in school," the older boy said.

Startled, Ethel's heart squeezed at the need evident in the child's simple statement. The school would not want to offer books to homeless children who might lose them or never bring them back. Tears stung the back of her eyes, but she smiled and nodded. "We'll see you soon," she promised.

True to her word, two days later she re-entered the shelter with George at her side. Jonathan, Sue, and the boys readily greeted them once again. This time, not only did she bring cookies, but she brought several wrapped packages.

Sue's eyes widened, and she shook her head. "Oh, Miss Ethel, you shouldn't have."

"It's just a little something," she said, lifting her thin shoulders. She watched with delight as the boys ripped off the paper, finding a small stack of books for each of them. Their awe was humbling, and she once again battled the sting of tears. Kneeling close by, she explained, "Most of these are fairy tales that I thought you'd enjoy. They're entertaining but can teach us so much about life."

Both boys threw their arms around her, almost knocking her over with their enthusiastic hug. She laughed and squeezed them tightly, joy filling her heart.

That evening, she and George sat in the living room, Christmas music once again playing softly from the radio and the lights from the tree casting the room in a holiday glow. The fire crackled from the fireplace, warming the room as they read.

"I know that was hard for you."

So deep into the story she was reading, George's voice cut through, the interruption causing her head to snap up and see him staring thoughtfully at her. "Hard for me?"

"Going by the shelter with the cookies and the books."

She slid a bookmark between the pages and closed her book, giving him her attention. "George, taking a simple gift to someone in need is hardly difficult."

He nodded slowly, his gaze turning toward the fireplace that cast his face in light and shadows. He had no trouble speaking his mind, but she knew that he was careful with his thoughts. With their books now resting in their laps, she waited as her stomach flip-flopped, unsure of the road his mind was traveling down.

"I wanted to give you children, Ethel," he began. She opened her mouth to refute the idea that he had somehow failed her, but his lifted hand stilled her words. "I know there's no saying exactly why God hasn't blessed us that way, but I know it sits heavy with you. You have so much love to give, Ethel. And I feel selfish because since we've been married, that love has rained down mostly on me. I know that being around those boys today made you think about what we don't have."

Her throat was clogged with unshed tears, and they were silent as they both swallowed deeply. He would make such a good father, thinking of all the ways he would've passed on his quiet goodness, intelligence, patience, and fun spirit. Dragging in a shaky breath, she said, "Yes, my sweet George, I wanted to give you children. We don't know that it's not going to happen, but I confess that every month, I feel the ache a bit deeper."

"I was always taught that God gives us what he wants us to have, not always what we think we deserve. But that doesn't mean that it's easy to accept."

Losing the battle to keep tears at bay, they slid down her cheeks, landing unheeded on the front of her blouse. She nodded slowly. "I've spent untold hours on my knees in prayer for children. Children I could raise, comfort, teach, guide, and love. I'm slowly coming to accept that might not happen for us. I'm also slowly coming to learn that there are other ways that I can reach out to children." She tried to smile but knew George could see straight through her.

He placed his book on the table next to him, stood, and moved closer before kneeling next to her. He lifted his large hand and swept her tears from her cheeks. "You are the prettiest girl I've ever seen, Ethel. And you're the strongest woman I've ever known. Don't ever doubt, no matter what happens, how much I love you."

Her book slid to the floor as she leaned forward, pulling his face toward hers. Their lips met in a kiss, soft and gentle, strong with an aching need. They celebrated their Christmas Eve the way they had for the past several years... alone, but together.

The next morning, she woke before George and lay in bed staring at her handsome, kindhearted husband. So as not to wake him, she whispered. *"Whatever life has in store for us, George, I promise to do whatever I can to honor you."*

Heart a little lighter, she slipped from bed, dressed quickly, and hurried downstairs. After all, she had a Christmas breakfast to make.

3

TEN YEARS LATER

In the midst of baking her multitude of cookies, Ethel kept an eye on the pot bubbling on top of the stove. The homemade chicken noodle soup was ready, and she slid it off the hot stove eye. Quickly pulling out the last batch of cookies, she placed them on the cooling rack and turned her attention back to the soup. Ladling large spoonfuls into a bowl, she sniffed appreciatively, satisfied that it was seasoned to perfection.

Hearing a noise behind her, she jerked around. "What are you doing down here? I was going to fix a tray and bring it up to you."

"With all you have to do, I'm not about to lay in bed like a lazy fool and have you serve me!" George said before a deep, rumbling cough interrupted his grumbling.

"You work too hard." Her words were scolding, but her tone was not. Having succumbed to a cold weeks ago, George had continued to work, wanting the men in his shop to take as much time off as they wanted throughout the holidays to be with their families. Right before Christmas, pneumonia had set in. He'd spent several days in the hospital as Ethel worried and fretted. Now he was home, recuperating and grumpy.

"Well, the last of my cookies are out of the oven, so let's sit in the dining room, and I'll eat with you." She didn't miss his satisfied smile as she turned back to the stove.

"You always were the best company, Ethel."

He carried their cups of hot tea into the dining room while she picked up the tray now loaded with two bowls of soup, homemade bread, and butter. As was their habit, they sat at one end of the large dining room table. George at the end, and she to his right.

He moaned in appreciation as the soup slid past his lips, complimenting her cooking. "This is delicious." He winked, adding, "Not as good as your fried chicken, but then nothing is."

Their meal was interrupted a few times with his coughing, and as she worried over him, she didn't voice her concern out loud. It had seemed several days ago that he was getting better, but now she was uncertain. A sheen of sweat covered his brow, and his skin was pale. Having always loved the holidays, she now wished that the weather was warmer and he could sit outside under a shade tree enjoying a warm spring day.

Once finished with their dinner, she escorted him to his comfortable chair in the living room and bent to kiss his forehead. "I'm going to rinse out the bowls, and I'll bring you some more hot tea." She turned to leave the room, then looked over her shoulder. "And I'll bring you a cookie."

Several minutes later, she reappeared and set another tray on the coffee table. Having liberally doused his hot tea with lemon and whiskey, she watched as he took a sip.

His brows lifted as his eyes widened. "Well, if this doesn't cure me, it'll certainly make me feel a lot better!"

She laughed and sat in her seat next to him, picking up her knitting needles from the basket at her feet.

"What are you making now?"

She held up a tiny knitted cap. "I heard from Judith Myers, who volunteers at the hospital, that the nursery needed smaller caps for the newborn babies that were premature. Some of the babies are so tiny that the regular caps the hospital provides are simply too big. I suggested to the church guild that those of us who could knit could make caps in the appropriate size." Her needles continued to click, but she was aware of George's gaze resting heavily on her. Finally looking up, she cocked her head to the side.

"You really are amazing, Ethel. Everything I ever wanted and everything I never knew I needed."

Her lips curved into a small but sad smile. "I can always tell when the thoughts hit you, George," she said. "Just because we weren't able to have children of her own didn't mean that we couldn't help others with theirs."

George had spent many hours over the years carving wooden toys that he would take to shelters and schools. Her holiday baking had spread throughout the year, and they often spent weekends handing out food to those in need.

A new round of coughing from George had him gripping the blanket she'd draped over his legs. Each sound ripped through her, and she desperately wanted to take away his illness. Once the coughing was under control, he leaned back in his chair, his breath carrying a new rattle.

"George, I was thinking that maybe this spring we could take a little trip. Perhaps go somewhere where the weather is very nice and warm—"

"I've made a decision about the shop, Ethel," he interrupted.

Surprised at the abrupt change in topic, she lay her needles in her lap and waited to see what he wanted to say.

"I know I'm not old, but this illness has made me realize that there are more things in life than just working six days a week. There was a time when I thought I could leave my business to a son or even a daughter. But instead of children, God gave me the most wonderful wife a man could ever have, and I want to make sure to take care of you."

They didn't speak often of the children they didn't have, knowing the time had passed for that particular blessing to be bestowed. But now, the pain of missed opportunities hit her once again. Swallowing deeply, she held his gaze, hoping he could feel all of her love spreading to him.

"My longest-serving employee, Fred, and I have talked about him becoming a partner. He's excited, has the money to buy me half-out, and that would give me a chance to ease some of the stress and spend more time with you."

Stunned, she had no doubt his intent was to offer her comfort, but his words sent a chill straight through her. Leaning forward, she placed her hand on his knee and gave a little squeeze. "What brought this on? Is it your illness? You'll get better, and gain your strength, and—"

"Not just this illness, Ethel. Certainly, the pneumonia has made me realize that I'm not going to live forever, but it's also giving me the idea that I should put some of my affairs in order. That's just smart business."

Her brow furrowed as she considered his words. "If you're doing this for me, George, please don't. If you're doing this for you because you need things to be easier on you, then that's what I want, too."

Holding her gaze, he explained, "I'm doing this for us. You and me, sweetheart. For us." When she didn't reply, he continued. "The shop is doing well, but if I let Fred buy out half the business, then that's money in the bank for us that's not tied up in the business. If something happens to me, that money would pay off this mortgage and allow you to continue living here."

"I don't like talking about this," she huffed.

He reached out his hand to cover hers that still rested on his leg. "Now, now, my sweet Ethel. You were the smartest as well as the prettiest girl I ever met. You know that to plan for the future... to plan for the inevitable only makes sense."

"I know," she said, her words barely above a whisper.

"But you're scaring me, as though this isn't far off into the future but as though you're planning for something much sooner."

"The only planning I'm doing is for the eventual day when I'm not here. My goal is to put that day off as long as I can, but I wouldn't be a good husband if I didn't look ahead to prepare so your life would still be good."

His words spoke to her sense of logical order and planning. *So why does my heart ache so badly right now?* She simply nodded, and he leaned back in his chair, a sigh of relief leaving his lungs.

"I'll talk to Fred tomorrow, and we'll make the arrangements. And then sometime, if he wants, he can buy out the business completely from me. I can still work occasionally, but that would allow for you and me to do the things we want to do. And then when something does happen to me, you wouldn't have to worry about the business and would have plenty of money."

She placed her knitting back into the basket at her feet. Standing together, they linked fingers and walked toward the staircase. She felt a pull on her hand and stopped, twisting her head to look up at George.

"I hate to kiss you with this awful cough, but we are under the mistletoe." He winked and added, "I've never once missed kissing you under the mistletoe in all these years."

She smiled and lifted her arms around his neck, kissing him lightly. Then, with arms encircling each other, they made their way up to the bedroom. Lying in bed, watching him sleep, she listened carefully for any rattling in his lungs. Finally, as sleep called her, she thought, *if life never gives me anything else but the blessings I've already received from being Mrs. George Wiseman, I would be an eternally happy woman.*

———

One year later

There was no fire in the fireplace. No wreath on the door. No Christmas tree in the corner of the room. The red tablecloth which always graced her dining room table during the holidays was still folded and in the cabinet. No candles were lit. No presents bought. The halls were not decked with greenery.

Christmas cookies had been baked, but they'd all been given away, none filling her own personal cookie jars.

It seemed a sin to not celebrate, but when all joy was gone, simply existing was hard enough.

Ethel's knitting needles perched quietly in the neglected ball of yarn in the basket at her feet. Her Bible was opened on her lap, her hands clasped together, resting on top of the pages. She drew in a deep breath, the air hitching as it reached her lungs before she let it out slowly.

Her gaze moved slowly about the room, noting its familiarity, and yet feeling as though a stranger in her own house. *House... it used to be a home. But no longer.* She whispered into the quiet room, "George..."

George's illness had lingered, damaging his lungs irrevocably, weakening his strong body, making him susceptible to more illness. He had moved forward with his plans, selling half the business to Fred while continuing to work for months as he was able. He finally sold the rest of the business, assuring Ethel there was money in the bank. She had waved her hand dismissively, insisting that as long as they were together, they'd have everything they needed.

Two months ago, she'd woken up in the middle of the night hearing George struggling to breathe. Remaining calm, she'd called for the rescue squad, then dressed quickly, racing to the hospital. A day later, she held his hand and soothed his brow as more deep coughs racked his body.

He had finally opened his eyes, focused on hers, and smiled. "My beautiful Ethel."

His voice was so soft, she'd had to lean close to hear his words.

"There's so much I wanted to give you. So much I wanted us to be able to do."

Shushing him, she'd said, "Oh, George, we have many years ahead of us to do all the things we want to do." She had watched as he slowly shook his head and she continued to smooth the sweat from his brow. "I have no purpose without you. You are my sole reason for living."

"That's my line, Ethel. My sole reason for living was you, and you have so much more life to live and life to give."

Her breath had halted in her lungs as she choked,

"Without you, there's nothing." She waited as another round of coughing caused the creases in his face to deepen in pain, and she silently prayed for his easing.

His eyes had fluttered open and closed and open once again. His lips had curved slightly as he whispered, "You have gifts far beyond anyone I've ever known, sweetheart. You'll find those who need your gifts. You'll seek out those who can only be saved by you."

She'd had no idea what his words meant and the idea of living her life without his love sliced her open, leaving her bleeding on the floor.

"I have to go, Ethel. But I promise I'll never be far away. I'll be in every breath you take and every beat of your heart. And when it's time... I'll be with you, waiting."

With his hands still gripped in hers, she stood and bent over the bed, her tears dripping from her cheeks onto his. Kissing his dry lips, she'd felt the instant life left his body.

That had been two months ago. The first few weeks she'd been surrounded. The women from the church came by with casseroles and cakes, so much food she'd never be able to eat it all. Finally dumping most of it into the garbage, guilt hit her, knowing George would've taken it to one of the shelters.

It was almost easier now that the initial well-wishers and grief-watchers had gone. A few weeks ago, she'd finally climbed from bed, cleaned the house, shopped, and put on a face for the outside world so that they'd be assured she was fine. But on the inside, she was anything but fine. Invitations to spend the holidays in other people's homes flowed in, but she turned them all down with a smile. A smile that held the agonizing pain still deep inside.

And now, her first Christmas Eve alone, her mind was filled with George, and good memories slid past as well as ones that caused a twinge in her heart.

With another shuddering breath, she finally looked down at the pages in front of her. She had been searching for passages on grief, taking heart in the words of comfort. The words of Corinthians seemed to enlarge on the page. *"Praise be to the God and Father of our Lord Jesus Christ, the father of compassion and the God of all comfort, who comforts us in all our troubles, so that we can comfort those in any trouble with the comfort we ourselves receive from God."*

Words whispered in the dark room again. "God, what comfort can I give others? I feel so empty, how can I have anything to offer?"

She waited to see if words would come back to her, but the room remained silent. Closing her Bible, she placed it gently on the table next to her, glancing at her full but now cold cup of tea. Carrying the delicate china to the kitchen, she rinsed out the cup, flipped off the light, and walked across the hall to the small bedroom. She had not been able to sleep in the bedroom she'd shared with George since he passed. Guilt hit her again that she hadn't donated his belongings to those in need. The room had stayed much as it was when he was living.

With the upstairs empty, a familiar anger sliced

through her again. *Such a waste. This house was supposed to have been filled with children.*

Pushing that thought away before she fell down the deep hole of anger, self-pity, and more questions God should answer, she went to bed, alone and lonely on Christmas Eve.

4

TWO YEARS LATER

Ethel welcomed her close friend, Judith, into her home, ushering her back toward the kitchen. "Come on in! I've been baking for two days, and I think I have enough."

Judith stepped into the kitchen, took one look at the counter, and exclaimed, "Ethel, you're a treasure!"

Waving her hand dismissively, Ethel shook her head. "Oh, goodness. Hardly! I feel like knitting and baking are such small things to do to help others."

Judith rolled her eyes as she tucked a strand of hair behind her ear. "You do much more than that, and you know it. You volunteer at the school, reading to little kids. You volunteer at the church, helping with the elderly. You volunteer at the library. You take your knitted blankets to the hospital. And you're still baking for the shelter."

Ethel knew those things were true but also knew the reason deep inside. She remained quiet but had no doubt Judith understood.

Reaching across the counter, Judith placed her hand

on Ethel's, squeezing slightly. "I sometimes feel as though you're in a race to stay busy so that you won't think so much about George."

She lifted her gaze and nodded slowly, staring at her friend. "Staying busy has been my saving grace."

"You know, you're still young—"

"Go no further," she rushed to say. "George was the only love of my life." Grateful when Judith remained silent, she smiled, and they began placing the multitude of plastic tubs into bags. Judith had recently come from one of the church guild meetings and filled Ethel in on all the latest gossip.

"And wait until I tell you about John and Carol Higgins! I just found out they finished a foster care program and plan on taking kids into their home!"

She had always admired John and Carol, but the news surprised her. "I thought they were going to travel now that their kids were off to college."

Shrugging, Judith replied, "They heard of the need for foster homes and decided that they wanted to open their house. They said there were needy kids that had no home. No one to care for them."

Her heart squeezed at the thought of unwanted and neglected or abused children. "You said they had to go through a program?"

"I'm not sure if it was through the state or social services, but yes, they had to go through a foster parent program to be certified. It sounded rather in-depth, and of course, their house had to be checked out. Personally, I can't imagine having someone come in and investigate my home, but then I also can't imagine a strange child living with me. I admire what they're doing, but," Judith shrugged, "it's certainly not for me."

Ethel accompanied Judith onto her front porch, offering her a hug. As Judith made her way down the front walk, she turned and glanced back at the house and smiled up at Ethel.

"This house is so big for you, Ethel. I hate to think of you all alone here. Have you ever thought about moving?"

Ethel lifted her gaze lovingly over the house that George had chosen for them. Smiling, she shook her head. "This is home. This is where I feel George every day." With a wave, Judith made it to her car, and Ethel turned and walked back through the wreath-covered door. There was no tree in the living room, but she'd placed some of her favorite decorations on display. It was easier to decorate this year as grief had moved through the stages toward acceptance.

Sinking into the deep cushions of her favorite chair, she picked up her knitting, the clicking of the needles familiar and comforting. It was easy to allow her thoughts to wander as her fingers worked, and Judith's words sounded out in the silence. *Needy. No home. No one to care for them.* She was not surprised when anticipated anger filled her as she thought of abandoned, abused, or neglected children. Dropping her knitting onto her lap, her gaze found the picture of George resting on the table nearby. "You would have given anything for children, and here some people have what we never had, and they throw it away!"

The cruel twist of fate had her toss the knitting back

into the basket and taking to her feet. Pacing the floor, she continued to rant about the injustices in the world, shaking her fist and crying loudly. Finally exhausted, she moved to the chair that George had always sat in, now looking around the room from what had been his perspective. The multitude of books they'd collected over the years filled the shelves. The upstairs held empty bedrooms and her dining room table held empty chairs.

"You have gifts far beyond anyone I've ever known, sweetheart. You'll find those who need your gifts. You will seek out those who can only be saved by you."

His words resounded loudly in the room, words spoken near the end. "What are you trying to tell me, George? That I'm supposed to open *our* home to children that were never *ours?*"

"You will seek out those who can only be saved by you."

His words were so clear to her but only served to squeeze her heart more. "What can I do by myself, George? Maybe this is something we could have done together, but me? Alone? What on earth could I offer these children?"

"A soft bed. A warm home. A listening ear. Hardy food. A sense of stability. Someone to love them."

"What do I know about being a mother? If it was not God's will for me to be a mother, how would I even know what to do?" she asked, throwing her hands up into the air.

"God never intended for you not to share your love. You have so much to offer."

The room once again grew silent, but Ethel didn't

move. She sat in the chair that allowed her to still catch a whiff of George's aftershave, tears rolling down her cheeks. Minutes turned into hours, and for the first time in her life, she did not seek her bed. Instead, she was still sitting in the chair as the morning light filtered through the curtains.

Dragging in a deep, cleansing breath, she let it out slowly. Pushing herself to stand, her body felt stiff, but she moved toward her bedroom. An hour later, she stood in front of the mirror and stared at her reflection. A light dusting of powder covered her face. Her graying hair was pulled back into a bun. She had chosen a pale blue shirtwaist dress with a thin belt around her waist. Whispering to her reflection, she said, "Okay, George, I'm going to do this. But I've got to know that I'm not in this alone."

"I'll be in every breath you take and every beat of your heart."

Hearing that promise once again and knowing that her beloved husband had never made a promise he didn't keep, she squared her shoulders as she picked up her purse and walked out the door. It was not long before she sat in the head social worker's office in the Department of Social Services.

"And how may I help you, Mrs. Wiseman?" the woman with the kind eyes asked.

"I'd like information on how to become a foster mother." She held her breath, uncertain what the social worker's response would be. When the woman's lips curved into a wide smile, Ethel breathed a sigh of relief. She glanced down, almost certain that George had reached out to hold her hand. *Thank you, my sweet husband.* Looking back up, she met the social worker's smile with one of her own.

Three Years Later

Sitting in her chair by the fire, Ethel smiled as she looked from her knitting toward the towheaded boy sitting on the sofa, his finger pointing to each word as he read aloud.

"The night... Max... wore his... wolf... suit and made... mischief of one kind..." He turned the page, "and another." Turning the page again, he read, "His mother called... him Wild Thing!"

Ethel felt certain that Zander would look up proudly, grinning at the fun story and brightly illustrated picture book, *Where the Wild Things Are* by Maurice Sendak. Instead, he stared at the page for a long moment, his forefinger still resting on the words. Giving him the silence needed to process his thoughts, she waited to see what he might say.

Finally, he lifted his gaze to hers, his brow furrowed. His voice was barely above a whisper as he said, "That's what they called me."

Her heart squeezed, knowing instantly what he was referring to. *A wild child.* That's what they called him.

Ethel had fostered a number of children, usually for

a couple of weeks only. But then the social worker called with a special case. "Mrs. Wiseman, in the last several years, you have already earned a reputation for being one of the best foster mothers we have. With each case, you've been able to love, and nurture, and reach out to so many of our short-term cases. Now, I'm coming to you because you're not only our last hope, but maybe the only one who can truly reach this child."

Alexander King. Eight years old. His mother was an alcoholic and a junkie who rarely remembered she had a child. When he was only six years old, a police officer had caught him sneaking around a grocery store, filling his pockets. Concerned, the police officer had noted the skinny child, his clothes ill-fitting and dirty, and his body unwashed.

Once Zander was convinced that he wasn't going to jail, he showed the policeman where he lived. Inside the dilapidated apartment, the officer discovered Zander's intoxicated and strung-out mother inside. The place was a wreck. There was no food in the kitchen, and Zander's bed was nothing but a blanket on the floor. The police officer took Zander into emergency custody and called social services.

Zander had been placed in temporary foster homes over the last couple of years, all excellent homes, but each time he ran away. The social worker discovered he'd never been in school and didn't know how to read. Running the streets at his young age was all he knew to do. In desperation, the social worker talked to Ethel, who agreed without hesitation to take him in.

Her one condition—she didn't want him to finish

out the school year, insisting that she would home-school him instead. When the social worker questioned her idea, Ethel had said, "I want school to be a place that he loves, and that's not going to happen right now. Give me several months to teach him to read and help him catch up with first-grade work. Then he can start with the next school year, confident in his abilities and eager to learn."

The social worker had warned Ethel that he might not be able to learn or would react negatively to being with her all the time. But Ethel knew that he would never enjoy school if he could not feel confidently successful. And her plan had worked… eventually.

While Zander had never tried to run away from her and easily succumbed to her loving kindness, he fought against learning how to read. But with children's books and fairytales, he quickly learned that reading was not an unattainable goal. And now, a year later, she waited to see what his thoughts were.

"I heard a teacher call me a wild child 'cause I didn't like to stay in my seat," he said. His face scrunched in thought. "I didn't like walking in a line. I didn't like being told when it was time to eat or when it was time to go play."

"That certainly didn't make you wild," she said, sniffing in irritation at his former teacher's words. "You were just very independent. There's nothing wrong with that, but we do have to adapt to some expectations." Leaning forward, she smiled as she held his gaze. "I think you're a wonderful little boy who's growing and learning every day."

As Zander seemed satisfied with her words, he went back to reading, and she cast her gaze around the room. A Christmas tree once again sat in the corner of the living room, the ornaments that she and George had purchased years before hung on its branches, proudly sharing space with the decorations she and Zander had made. A fire once again crackled in the fireplace. Books still lined the shelves, now filled with children's classics as well. That evening, she and Zander had sat at the red-clothed table eating their dinner, her heart swelling with pride as his feet swung back and forth in the chair, his body finally relaxed and easy as they shared a meal.

"And Max... the King of all wild things was lonely... And wanted to be where... someone loved him... best of all."

Her gaze dropped back to the towheaded boy, who now looked at her with eyes filling with moisture. "I know how he feels."

The words were whispered, but each punctuated with overwhelming emotion. She opened her arms, and Zander dropped the book and rushed over. He was getting larger with good food in his body, but she still held him in her lap as he sobbed against her shoulder.

Rocking him back and forth, she comforted, "My dearest boy. My dearest Alexander. You are so brave, so kind, and so smart. I'm in awe of you every day." He lifted his head and his watery gaze stared up at her. "And never forget how much I love you."

As his thin arms encircled her neck, he whispered into her ear, "I love you too, Miss Ethel."

Holding him tight, she blinked as her own tears slid

down her cheeks. After a moment, she said, "Do you think it's time to get Santa's cookies and milk ready?"

Leaning back again, Zander swiped at his cheeks and grinned while nodding with enthusiasm. He slid from her lap, and hand-in-hand they walked to the kitchen, the sound of carols from the radio following their footsteps.

After he was tucked into bed with promises of an early Christmas morning, she walked back downstairs to tidy the room. She tucked a few presents under the tree, took a bite from one of the cookies, and drank the small glass of milk. Suddenly overwhelmed, she dropped back into her chair, closing her eyes tightly against the wave of emotions crashing against her.

Opening her eyes, she gasped slightly at the sight of George now sitting on the sofa, his hand resting on the discarded book.

"I always knew you'd be the best, my sweet Ethel. And here you are, living proof."

"I sometimes feel very lost, George. How do I know that I'm able to meet all of his needs?"

"You were the oldest of six. You helped raise your younger siblings."

"His needs are much greater," she reminded. "Sometimes it's very hard."

"'It's when you know you're licked before you begin, but you begin anyway and see it through no matter what.' At least that's what Atticus Finch said."

She could not help but smile. "You always did like Harper Lee's *To Kill a Mockingbird*." She sighed, her gaze holding tightly onto the face she missed so much. "But you're right. Truthfully, Zander makes it very easy to see this through. He is so loving."

"He is loving, but it took you to teach him what true love is. Just like you taught me."

They were silent for a moment before she dragged in a ragged breath and knew that he would soon be gone. "I still miss you, you know," she said even though the words were unnecessary.

He smiled, and just like the first time, the sight warmed her heart. *"I promise I'll never be far away. I'll be in every breath you take and every beat of your heart."*

She closed her eyes, thanking God for another chance to share a moment, allowing unending love to pass between them. When she opened her eyes, the room was once again still and silent, the twinkling of Christmas lights sending shards of color about the space. Smiling, she stood and headed to bed, knowing the next morning would come early as the house would fill with Zander's laughter.

5

TWO YEARS LATER

Ethel glanced at the clock on the stove and hurried to take out the next batch of cookies. Wiping her hands on her apron, she just had time to throw open the front door, her gaze falling warmly upon the three boys bounding toward the house.

Zander, growing tall and strong, his Nordic heritage showing with his deep-set blue eyes and blonde hair. He had blossomed under her tutelage during the time needed for just the two of them. But now, he fell into the role of older brother with ease, loving the sense of family she was trying so hard to instill.

Rafe Walker followed Zander, his dark hair swept to the side. He had been with her for a year. When his parents had been killed and grief threatened to overwhelm the young boy, she readily opened her arms when the social worker called. Never wanting to replace what he had lost, she instead surrounded him with love, offering him a new family. A year younger than Zander,

Rafe had taken to the love she'd offered, and the two boys had formed a close bond.

Zander immediately wanted to share a room with Rafe, so she'd added bunk beds to one of the larger bedrooms, making it easy several months later when she acquired Cael Holland, adding to the brotherhood. His father had been killed while serving with the military, and his mother fell into grief, neglecting her children. His grandmother tried to help but was too infirm to handle the young boy, so she only kept his older sister. The social worker had not wanted Cael to be shuffled amongst families, and Ethel eagerly opened her arms when asked. The same age as Rafe, the three boys had become inseparable.

As they bounded into the house, each throwing their arms around her in turn, she greeted them warmly.

"Last day of school before the holiday break!" Cael called out, his arms raised high in a sign of victory.

"I got an A on my reading test," Zander said, his manner calmer than Cael's, but she saw the bright spark of excitement and pride in his eyes.

"I aced my math test and got four Christmas cards from girls in my class," Rafe said. His nose wrinkled, and he shook his head. "Girls... who can figure them out?"

Laughing, she welcomed them into the house. "Go on back to the kitchen. The Christmas cookies for you all are in the Santa tin. The others will be packed to take to the shelters once they are cool. Zander, you pour the milk, and Cael, you grab the napkins."

They were soon sitting at the table, decorated with

the red cloth and greenery in the middle, sharing a snack and more tales of their school day. Rafe was still complaining about the girls who had given him Christmas cards.

Ethel stifled her grin, noting his ready smile, and knew that in a few years he'd have even more female attention. That thought caused her to inwardly grimace. "Girls mature faster than boys do. They offer you cards to gain your attention. One day, you'll be appreciative."

"As long as I've got my brothers, that's all I'll need," Rafe said, shoving another cookie into his mouth.

She lifted her brow, and he immediately swallowed, taking a sip of milk.

"I'm sorry, Miss Ethel. It's been a long time since lunch."

She worked to instill manners in each of them but smiled indulgently. "Well, you boys certainly are growing, that's for sure." All three were tall, with the gangly preteen bodies that she knew held the promise of handsome men. Zander had already gained in height and weight, and she had no doubt his father was probably a big man. Rafe was not far behind, but Cael, as the tallest with a shock of red hair and an easy-going personality, was her steady rock amongst the three.

As they finished their snack and rinsed the dishes, she said, "Since the holidays are upon us and you don't have any homework, I'm going to suggest a reading challenge."

"Challenge?" Zander asked, his brow lifted. He had become an ardent reader, often reading at night to the others. The large book of fairy tales she had given him was well-read and beloved.

She laughed at his eager expression. "Whatever else you choose to read, find at least one holiday or winter story. It can even be a children's story for those younger than you, but one that's new to you."

That night, after the boys had listened while Zander read before falling asleep, she sat in her chair, her knitting neglected at her feet. She closed her eyes, not surprised to hear George's greeting whispering through the room.

"You're worried, my sweet Ethel."

She nodded, opening her eyes and seeing him standing near the tree. A slight rustling of one of the ornaments let her know he was thinking of the many times they'd decorated together. Sighing, she said, "I can't imagine my life without them, but perhaps it was a mistake for me to take boys. I might've helped with my younger siblings when my parents were busy, but my father made sure my brothers knew how to grow into good men. I'm suddenly faced with the realization that I might not have all that it takes to do this."

"I think you're selling yourself short."

She shook her head slowly. "Not at all. I'm being realistic. I'm a middle-aged, single woman who never had children of my own. I now have three boys who, in the not too distant future, will become young men. They'll be ready to enter a whole new world... everything from sports to their own physical maturity, and that includes dating." She offered an indelicate snort as she smiled. "Do I need to remind you that I fell in love with you at sixteen? That hardly makes me an expert on dating and relationships."

George chuckled, rocking back and forth on his toes with his hands behind his back. *"My dear, do what you've always told Zander to do. Break a problem down into smaller, more manageable pieces. Yes, your boys are growing older. As far as sports, they'll have coaches and teammates. There's no rule that says you have to be the one to get out and throw the ball to them. And as far as the other? What better way to teach them to be men than to teach them how to treat you and others? They respect you, therefore they are learning to respect women. And as far as relationships, again, the way they treat you, they'll have no problem transferring that to someone else they love."*

"My, my, George. You do have all the answers tonight." She smiled and leaned back in her chair.

After a moment of gentle silence, he spoke again. *"That's not all, is it? The phone call you received earlier is preying upon your mind."*

Sighing, she nodded slowly. "It's good now, with just three boys. They're used to each other. Confident. Secure. I'm not sure I should consider more."

"Twin boys. After their mother died, bounced from grandmother to aunt, and now unwanted because of the aunt's new husband. Tragic. Especially if they're separated."

Her gaze jumped from her clasped hands in her lap up to George. "Are you trying to guilt me, George Wiseman?"

He smiled sadly but shook his head. *"I would never try to guilt a woman who gives as much of herself as you do, my sweet Ethel. I also would never want to burden you with more than you can handle. But you have such love. It flows straight from God through you with such abundance. If you're worried about Zander, Rafe, and Cael, they'll learn openhearted acceptance and be the better man because of it."*

The silence descended upon the room once again, the crackling of the fire the only noise. Her lips slowly curved, and she said, "Well, it looks like my little family is going to expand again." Holding his gaze, she felt the piercing straight through her heart when she added, "I only wish that you were here with me."

"I am. And that's how I know you'll be fine."

A week later, on Christmas Eve, five boys settled around the living room with Ethel. She needn't have worried about Jaxon and Jayden... the other boys enveloped them into the fold. A year younger than Rafe and Cael, they adapted quickly to the changes. It did not take her long to realize the twins gained strength from each other, and she never doubted again the decision to take them on. There were other excellent foster parents who were short-term only, but she couldn't imagine not having all her boys.

"Jaxon, Jayden, before you came to live with us, I had given a challenge to the others to share a holiday story that they'd read." She smiled and nodded toward Cael and Rafe, who entertained them as they acted out 'Twas The Night Before Christmas.

When it was Zander's turn, he grinned, puffing out

his chest. "I found something," he said. "A story that I'm not sure you've heard of before, Miss Ethel."

Clasping her hands in her lap, her eyes twinkled as she held his gaze. "I'm intrigued! What do you have for us?"

"The Little Girl and the Winter Whirlwinds. It's by an unknown Bulgarian author."

Settling back into her chair, she sipped her tea as the others downed their cups of hot chocolate. With eager expressions, everyone's attention focused on Zander as he read of the tale about a Winter Witch who decided to keep spring from coming and a small village in the mountains who needed someone to travel to the highest mountain peak to ask Father Winter for help.

"A little orphan girl who lived with her grandfather volunteered for the journey, claiming she had a warm heart that would protect her. Her friends gave her a coat, scarf, mittens, and boots, making sure she was dressed appropriately for the trip. The winds began to whip and whirl around her, attempting to keep her from her mission. But her heart kept her warm, and she continued until the winds tired. The winds called upon the blizzards which became very angry and threw themselves down on her. Once again, she prevailed and the blizzards became tired.

"They called upon their mother, the Wicked Witch, who was very cunning. She appeared as a beautiful woman in a white dress with ice crystals like diamonds. She enticed the young girl to rest, not realizing she would fall asleep forever.

"Suddenly, a tiny mouse popped out from the snow

and realized the little girl was beginning to die. She called for her friends, and more mice came to rescue her, warming her hands and feet. Too small to get her warm enough, they called for their friends, the rabbits and squirrels, spreading their warmth over her. Soon, she awoke. They decided to go with her to Father Frost because they were cold as well. At the top of the mountain, they found the Ice Palace where Father Frost was sleeping. Waking him, they told him of their plight. He blew his whistle and called for the Winter Witch to be brought to him where he could lock her into the cellar until it was time for the next winter. Once that was done, the sun began to shine and the snow melted in the warmth. Everyone cheered the brave little girl when she returned home."

At the end of the story, Ethel clapped her hands and exclaimed, "I have never heard of that story before, Zander! Where on earth did you find it?"

He blushed and shrugged as he mumbled, "I simply searched for a book on rare holiday tales and found this one."

Cael looked over at her and said, "I know what you're going to ask us. You want to know what the story can teach us."

She nodded, not surprised the older boys expected that. Looking toward Jaxon and Jayden, she said, "Many fairy tales of old were often told as a way to teach lessons. I know that Zander has been reading to you before you go to bed, and I'm sure you've noticed that the older boys like to talk about the stories they read. It's important to dig deep into the stories." She spread her hands out wide and smiled. "I think there's a lot in that story we can learn."

"Just because you're little doesn't mean you can't do things," Rafe said. "That little girl was braver than the grown-ups."

"And the other people in the village helped her," Cael added. "They gave her warm clothes to wear on her trip."

Jaxon and Jayden were sitting next to each other on the floor, and she watched as Zander leaned down and softly asked, "What about you? Would did you like about the story?"

The twins looked at each other, and for a moment she thought they weren't going to answer. Then Jayden grinned, and said, "I like how the little animals—"

"Even the really little ones, like the mice," Jaxon interjected.

"—were able to help her," Jayden finished.

Laughing, Ethel clapped her hands, pride filling her heart. "All of you are so right! Even the little animals were able to save her. And her friends helped take care of her. And she was so brave to want to help her village."

Zander caught her eye and smiled. "Kinda like us."

Nodding slowly, her eyes twinkled. "Yes, my dears. Exactly like us. A lesson that even I needed to remember."

"You?" Rafe's mouth dropped open in surprise. "But you're old—" His words halted as Zander reached over and poked him in the shoulder. "Um… I mean… um… older…"

She laughed again and said, "You are exactly right. I

am older. But that doesn't mean that I can't learn things."

"What did you learn, Miss Ethel?" Jaxon asked.

Casting her fond gaze amongst the five boys, she said, "I'm learning to be brave, even when I doubt myself. I'm learning that we can all, in our little family, take care of each other. And I've definitely learned that each of us has an infinite amount of love to give."

That night, after kissing each boy a good night and tucking them in with individual words of wisdom just for them, she made her way back downstairs. Turning out the house lights and lamps, the Christmas tree was the only thing sending shards of color about the room. She didn't need to turn around to know that George was there.

"Thank you," she whispered.

"I never doubted you for a moment, my dear Ethel. Do you finally now believe that you have enough love to give?"

She nodded slowly. "Yes, I believe together we are stronger than one." She felt the slight movement of air in the room and knew that George's presence had left for the moment. She also had no doubt that he would reappear anytime she needed him.

As she moved to the bedroom on the first floor where she continued to take up residence, she said aloud, "Yes, together we are stronger than one." That was why, a year later, another little boy sat on her living room floor listening to stories. Her quiet little Asher, having been abused, was welcomed into their home by her and the other boys.

6

FIVE YEARS LATER

The boys were on their way home from school, and Ethel finished sorting the laundry. Eight plastic baskets lined the table across from the large load washer and dryer. *Eight.* Her house was filled to capacity with laughter and love abounding, mixed in with the occasional squabble.

A few emergency placements had come and gone, but besides her six boys, she'd added two more to her loving family. Zeke came to her at the age of thirteen, when Zander was seventeen. A kind, goodhearted young man, he was afraid of becoming as angry and abusive as his father had been. He relished the time with the older teens, developing a camaraderie with them he'd never felt with his birth home.

Castiel was the last one to join them, a quiet, introspective, artistic teenager. His carvings amazed her, and she had no doubt he would continue to work with wood the way his father had. Like the others, he bonded quickly.

Just as she finished the sorting, a knock on the door surprised her, and she walked toward the front of the house. Opening her front door, she spied a tall man, his glasses perched on his hawked nose as he peered down at her. To his side stood Mrs. Barker, one of the social workers that had placed a few of the boys with her. Prickles of concern moved through her as she saw the man's narrowed-eyed gaze and Mrs. Barker's lips pinched into a thin line.

"Mrs. Barker, how may I help you?"

"Good afternoon, Mrs. Wiseman. This is—"

"I'm Wallace Smith, assistant to the director of the Department of Social Services. We are here to do an unannounced inspection of your home."

"Okay," she agreed, "but I need to ask you to step aside for just a moment."

"I won't step aside for anyone—"

"Miss Ethel!" came the shout from the boys as they jogged up the front walk, backpacks slapping against her shoulders.

"I'm afraid you will step aside," Ethel continued, "at least until I've had a chance to greet my boys." It appeared that Mr. Smith was not going to move until he turned around and saw the size of the boys. All large, tall, well-built, athletic. He jumped out of the way as though afraid of them, his glare evident as they nodded toward him and Mrs. Barker but headed directly to Miss Ethel. Hugs and warm greetings ensued, and she ushered them inside. "Boys, please get your snacks and take them to the dining room."

The boys headed down the hall to do her bidding, but Zander held back, his protective gaze landing on her. Patting his arm, she said, "It's okay, Zander. Mrs. Barker and Mr. Smith are here today for an unannounced inspection." Zander narrowed his eyes on them but obediently followed his brothers down the hall.

Turning back to her visitors, she said, "Please, come in. I'm used to my annual visits but wonder if there's a particular reason for this unscheduled one."

"When I took charge and was reviewing cases, I was shocked to see that a single woman—a woman of your age—was attempting to raise eight boys! Eight! I immediately questioned Mrs. Barker and was told that the situation here was well in hand and considered one of the best in the city." Looking down at her he sneered. "Somehow, I doubt that. I would say the money you get for being a foster parent of eight children is what keeps you taking these boys in."

Forcing her voice to remain calm, she replied, "You've seen the size of my boys, Mr. Smith. I doubt they would be fed so well if I only relied on the money that came in from the state." Before he had a chance to speak again, she added, "But I welcome you into my home. Please, look around."

"We will!" Mr. Smith pushed his way inside.

Mrs. Barker stepped forward and whispered, "I'm so sorry!"

"It's fine," Ethel assured, but she wished her heart would not beat so loudly. One word from this man, and she knew one or more of her boys could be taken from her.

"I'll inspect the upstairs first," he announced, and his leather shoes tapped a harsh pattern on the wooden stairs. Mrs. Barker hurried after him, and Ethel turned to see all of her boys standing in the hallway, their expressions a mixture of shock, anger, and fear.

Before she had a chance to reassure them, Zander spoke. "Someone complained, didn't they?"

Forcing her voice to remain steady, she said, "No, I don't think that's what happened. Mr. Smith is new to the supervisory job at the Department of Social Services and was simply surprised to see that eight boys are living here."

Zeke's hands flexed into fists, and she captured Zander's gaze and slightly jerked her head toward the younger boy. "I need all of you to remain calm, let them do their inspection job, and they'll see what a wonderful place we have together."

"I don't want to go anywhere else," Asher said, his voice shaky. He tugged on the long sleeves covering his gangly arms, always hiding the cigarette burn scars from years of abuse from his mother's boyfriend when he was younger.

He had come so far in learning to trust her and the other boys, she felt fury moving through her over Asher's concerns. She knew he was only voicing her own fears, but she refused to give into them. Stepping closer, she placed her hand on his shoulder. "My dear boy, let's not jump to conclusions. But always believe, I'll fight to the death to keep my family together."

Lifting her gaze back to Zander, she was glad when he accepted her silent command and herded the other boys into the dining room. Turning, she hurried up the stairs and remained in the hall as Mr. Smith moved through the bedrooms.

"My oldest, Zander, has a room to himself. It has a private bathroom, but he readily shares it with anyone who needs it. The other two bedrooms are quite large, easily accommodating the bunk beds, as you can see. The closets are also large, and the chests of drawers are shared.

With the two large bedrooms upstairs, she'd placed bunk beds and a single into the rooms, allowing for the six boys. Zander, Rafe, and Cael filled one, and Jaxon, Jayden, and Asher filled the other. When Zeke joined them, she'd offered Zander the smaller room where he would not have to share his space with the others since he was the oldest and had Zeke take Zander's bed. When Cas came along, she'd added another bunk to the younger boys' bedroom. In one of her many conversations with George, he had assured her that the boys would bond into a brotherhood with the shared space.

The rooms were so familiar to her, but she tried to look at them through new eyes. The furniture was slightly worn but clean, and the beds were covered with warm comforters and firm pillows. A bookcase stood in the corner, filled with the books that they were currently reading or wanted to have close at hand.

Mr. Smith lifted the mattress of one bed and peered underneath, finding nothing.

"May I ask what you're looking for?"

"Cigarettes. Drugs. Pornographic magazines."

A gasp left her lips, and she blinked in surprise. "If the boys were smoking cigarettes, I would smell it. They care too much about their health for smoking or drugs."

He stood and sneered, once again staring down at her. "And pornography?"

"I assume you think that I, being an older woman, know nothing about pornographic magazines." Her lips curved slightly, and she said, "My boys are normal and healthy, and I have no doubt that they have an interest in what others might pass around at school. But if they choose that particular reading material, I hardly doubt they would bring it into my house. There's a level of respect we have for each other."

Not finding anything untoward in the room, he pushed past her and walked across the hall, finding an almost identical room. Giving it the same scrutiny, he then moved to Zander's room after inspecting the bathroom at the end of the hall.

"Eight boys and only one bathroom?"

"Since I've already stated that Zander's room stays open and is welcome for anyone, there are two full bathrooms up on the second floor for the eight boys. I have my own bedroom and bathroom downstairs and there's a powder room as well. So, two showers, three toilets, and multiple sinks in the house have not proven too few for the boys to share. I dare say our servicemen and women in the military have less."

"I wouldn't know about that," he retorted.

Her lips twitched. "I didn't think you would." She caught his look of irritation and choked back the words that wanted to fly out. It was evident he was on a mission. A mission to find some reason to take any of her boys from her.

She felt a hand on her shoulder and a whisper in her ear. "Stay calm, Ethel. All will be well." Recognizing George's voice, she inhaled deeply before letting her breath out slowly.

Leading the social workers back downstairs, she led them past the dining room where the large table was filled with the boys whose expressions still ranged from anger to fear. The anger she could deal with later, but the fear only amplified hers.

Following Mr. Smith into the kitchen, she observed as he opened the refrigerator, finding it filled with milk, juice, vegetables, meat, and cheese. She opened her pantry door, exposing its packed contents of food as well. "I also have a freezer in the laundry room, where I occasionally will cook a meal ahead of time, especially if the boys have a variety of sporting or school events to attend."

"This is all very impressive," Mrs. Parker said. Casting a glare toward Mr. Smith, she added, "Just as I have always reported."

Taking a look into the laundry room, he glanced over his shoulder toward Ethel. "Who handles all this?"

"I usually do the washing, and each boy is tasked with putting his own clothes away. And before you ask about outdoor chores, all the boys share in the mowing, but the flower gardens responsibilities are mine, shared with Rafe."

With him still glowering, they walked back toward

the front of the house, passing the dining room once again. Once in the living room, he looked around, carefully walking past the wall of bookshelves filled with books of every kind.

She felt another presence at her back, but this time it was not George. That was confirmed when Zander spoke, "We sit in here every night and read. And discuss. Discuss books, what we read, what our dreams are. Each of us came from a place that was not so good, but landing here was the greatest gift we could have been given."

Tears pricked her eyes, but she could see Mr. Smith was not impressed. The boys formed a wall behind her, and she battled back her tears, praying for strength.

"I have concerns about eight boys living together. If they get out of hand, how would you ever be able to control them?"

"I don't have to control them," she bit back. "I love them, care for them, and respect them. That's what I've taught them, and that's what I get in return. That's what they get from each other."

"Mrs. Parker, you know," Cael said, turning toward the social worker. He towered over her but managed to keep his intimidation in check. "Why are you letting this happen?"

"It's not her decision, it's mine. Mine alone," Mr. Smith interjected. "And if I'm not satisfied that this house is the right place for you, I can have you removed."

The blasting heat of anger from behind her radiated

out, and Ethel lifted her hands gently to the side, knowing the boys would follow her lead.

Another knock at the door sounded, and her heart pounded even more. Before she had a chance to send one of the boys to see who it was, the door opened slightly.

"Miss Ethel?"

Turning, she saw one of her long-time neighbors and former close friend of George, who lived down the street. Smiling, she called out, "Judge Nelson, what can I do for you?"

"It was the strangest thing," he exclaimed. Stepping inside the house, he greeted the boys by name, and they, in turn, politely greeted him. Turning toward Ethel, he continued, "I was in my toolshed and suddenly remembered that your George had given me a chisel when I was determined to learn how to make table legs. I suddenly thought about your young Cas and thought he might like to come over sometime and give it a try." He looked at Cas and added, "I know you're particularly good with woodwork, and it was never a gift of mine. If you'd like to try it, I'll be more than happy to let you set it up over here. It belonged to my good friend and Ethel's husband, George, so it really belongs here."

"Mr. Smith, have you met Judge Nelson, my friend and neighbor?" Ethel asked.

"Um... no... um..." he stammered.

"Judge Nelson has assisted in making sure my boys are well taken care of."

The judge turned toward Mr. Smith and Mrs.

Barker. With a wide smile, he said, "Oh, are you visiting Miss Ethel? Best foster home in the city, I can tell you that! I've known her for more years than I care to count. Knew her husband, too." Looking back at Ethel, he said, "Like I said, it was the damnedest thing. It was as though George just came to me this afternoon and said that I needed to go have a chat with Ethel and the boys. So, here I am."

"Cas, why don't you and the others take the judge back to the dining room and offer him something to eat and drink? I'll be along shortly." She waited as her boys dragged their feet, evident that they preferred staying with her. Once they were all down the hall, she turned back to Mr. Smith. "I realize that in your position you see many heartbreaking situations. Some children have backgrounds similar to a few of my boys. Others, foster families that are not offering their homes and lives for the right reasons. I don't resent you coming here to find out about me and my boys. I can't control what you decide to do, but I will let you know that I will never give up these boys. They will tell you that I saved them... but, quite the contrary. They have given me a new lease on life."

"We're family," Rafe declared.

She startled at the sound of his voice close behind her. Turning, she saw the anguish on his face and reached out, placing her hand on his arm. He jerked at her touch, his gaze swinging from Mr. Smith to hers. "Sweetheart—"

"No, Rafe's right," Cael said. "I thought social

services was supposed to help kids, not split up families. We *are* a family."

"Would you be doing a search of the house if we were all related by blood?" Zander asked, his words hard and clipped.

"We know a family that had six kids," Jaxon piped up. "And their grandparents live with them, too, so they had a lot of people in that house. I bet you never went in there to snoop around."

Asher, pale and visibly shaking, slid in front of Cael. His eyes darted to Miss Ethel's, and he almost lost the battle to keep from crying. "She's Mom. She wanted me when my real mom didn't. You can try to take me away, but I'll always come back."

Heart threatening to rip into pieces at the emotions pouring from her boys, she whirled back around, stepped toe to toe with Mr. Smith, and shook her finger under his nose. "Mr. Smith, you are no longer welcome in my home. You do what you have to do, but remember, if you try to separate this family, I'll fight you every step of the way. I'll bleed and die until my boys are all safely under my roof again."

"Now, now, I'm sure no one's thinking about separating this family," Judge Nelson said as he walked back into the room, his hand gently resting on their shoulders as he maneuvered between the boys.

Her stomach was in knots, but she had known the judge for many years. On the outside easy-going and fun-loving, but he ruled his courtroom, often putting blowhard attorneys to shame. She recognized the firm statement he was making in spite of the smile on his face.

"No, no," Mr. Smith said, shaking his head emphatically, his eyes wide as he stared at the judge. "I never meant to imply that I was going to separate the family. It is a large group of boys, and we do have to be sure. I think from now on Mrs. Barker can make her annual visits." With that, he offered a short nod and made his way quickly out the front door. Mrs. Barker grinned and winked at the others before following him out.

Shaking, Ethel stood in silence, staring at the door. Judge Nelson patted her arm and said, "Funny thing, George coming to whisper in my ear today, don't you think?" With a nod, he followed the social workers out as well.

Choking back a strangled sob she tried valiantly to quell, she pressed her fingers to her lips. Zander's hand clasped her waist as he assisted her to her chair. Dropping into the seat as her shaky legs gave out, she quickly grabbed a tissue and wiped her eyes. The boys rushed to her, gathering around, most plopping awkwardly onto the floor at her feet while Zander and Rafe perched on the arms of her chair.

"I'll get you a cup of tea," Zeke said, hopping up.

"I'll be fine... I'm so sorry," she stammered, her face flaming as she reached out to place her hand on his arm. "Stay, please."

Forcing her breath to ease in and out of her lungs, she remained silent for a moment until her hands no longer shook. The reality that no one was taking them from her slowly settled into her mind, allowing her body to relax slightly.

"I couldn't believe how you stepped right up to him," Jayden said. Pressing his lips together, he stared up at her.

Jaxon piped up, "And shook your finger at him. You don't even do that with me!"

"That was the greatest!" Zeke enthused, his smile wide.

"I'm so sorry you boys had to witness that."

"Miss Ethel," Rafe said, his voice soft. "You can't keep all the bad stuff away from us."

"Sometimes you have to show force," Cael said, shifting slightly.

"No one's ever done that for me," Asher whispered, his eyes wide. "No one's ever fought for me before."

Her breath hitched, and she opened her arms, welcoming him as he flung himself into her embrace. She settled her gaze over their concerned faces. "I always wanted to show you boys that remaining calm and talking was the best way to handle every situation that arises."

"'Anybody can become angry—that's easy; but to be angry with the right person, and to the right degree, and at the right time, and for the right purpose, and in the right way—that is not within everybody's power and is not easy.' Miss Ethel, you've never taken the easy road," Zander said.

Her lips curved into a smile as she stared up at Zander. "Aristotle, I believe."

His grin met hers, as did the other boys'. "Aristotle... and me."

67

As the tension left the room, she looked toward the door and saw George standing nearby. Once more, he'd sent help when she was most in need, and her heart swelled. Mouthing *'thank you'*, she watched him nod, cast his gaze over the boys, and wink just before he drifted away.

7

FOUR YEARS LATER

The years passed far too quickly. Ethel still felt young at heart thanks to her wonderful boys, but she noticed new twinges nowadays, pains that didn't use to bother her.

When people discovered she had eight boys, all now teenagers, they clucked with amazement, shook their heads as though she'd lost her mind, or attempted to pour accolades on her. She cared for none of their reactions.

This evening, the house was unusually quiet, but as soon as the boys returned from the church Christmas party, the rooms would once again be filled with laughter. Over the years, she'd continued baking cookies for the party, this year giving them to the boys, glad that they had wanted to go.

She poured a cup of tea and walked into the living room, settling into her chair. The area underneath the tree was filled with presents. The next day, each of the boys would choose one of their gifts that they had been given, and they would all take them to one of the shelters. Smiling, it was a tradition that had been suggested by Zander years before.

As she sipped her tea, her gaze traveled about the room, noting it seemed so much like it had for the past thirty years. Volumes of well-read books lined the bookshelves but now were intermingled with silver picture frames containing photographs of all the boys. Seeing one where they were lined up with their arms around each other celebrating a baseball win, her heart warmed. George had been right. Excellent coaches had provided instruction, guidance, and lessons to each of them and they excelled in a variety of sports.

With a loving home, comfortable beds, and full bellies, they'd each grown beyond her expectations. She chuckled as she wondered over all the meals she'd cooked for the eight boys throughout the years.

George had also been right about her ability to guide them to manhood. She had given them respect and taught them how to respect her in return, which they each did in abundance. Making sure they knew the way to treat others, she'd seen the evidence over the years of the kind of men they were becoming. Loyal. Kindhearted. Willing to fight for what was right and stand up for others.

Her thoughts turned to Zander and his decision to join the Army six months after he graduated from high school. She winced at the thought, remembering George having done the same. Opening her eyes, she smiled as she saw George move into the room and once again stand by the Christmas tree.

He looked over and met her smile. *"I didn't mean to startle you, my dear. But your thoughts were so close to the surface, reminding me of days gone by."*

I was just thinking about when you were in the Army," she said. "I was absolutely sure my heart would break until you came back to me."

"My, my, that was a lifetime ago, wasn't it?" A knowing smile graced his face. *"I know you'll miss Zander horribly."*

She swallowed past the lump that appeared in her throat as tears pricked her eyes. "I can't imagine my life without him in it." Her heart squeezed. "But then, I couldn't have imagined my life without you."

"Oh, my dear Ethel, he'll always be with you."

She nodded, understanding the words he was saying, but she'd lived through something George had not—she'd been forced to live through the agonizing pain when someone you love is physically taken from you. With watery eyes, she looked at him and said, "I discovered I was strong enough to open my heart and home to my boys. I'm not sure I'm strong enough to let them go. I did that once with you. I don't want to do it again."

"Ah, the plight of every parent."

He sighed, and she was sure she felt his breath brushing across her face. The air rushed from her lungs as she hastened to say, "Oh, my dear, here I am complaining, and yet I've been given what you have not. The gift that slipped through our fingers together has been mine to carry and love."

His gaze was so intent that she could swear it was real. He reached over, and she imagined his fingers touched hers. *"But I did have this. I did get to be a father with you. Not in the way we thought. Not in the way we'd hoped for and prayed for. Not in the way that most people would understand or imagine. But throughout these many years, I've walked with you. Because of you, I've been given the greatest gift of all. It started with your love but continued when you never believed that death could separate us. You continued to allow me to come into your life. So yes, my sweet girl, you've allowed me to be a father."*

Tears slid down her cheeks, but she smiled. "Between you, me, and God, we've managed just fine, haven't we?"

"We've more than managed. Many children have felt your hand on their life, but our eight boys have had their lives completely changed. But all parents at some time have to realize that while their work is never done, they must send their children out into the world."

"But what if they need me?"

"You're not going anywhere. They'll come back to you. Trust in the power of love."

The sound of a car door closing startled her, and she glanced at the clock, shocked that an hour had passed. Looking over, she could no longer see George in the room, but she smiled. His presence was always with her. She barely had a chance to stand before the front door opened and eight smiling, exuberant, talking boys poured into the vestibule. The sight sent a thrill through her, one she hoped she never forgot. The day was coming when the house would be still and silent, so she wanted to treasure each moment that it was filled with laughter and love, talking and teasing, learning and living. "Oh, my, it sounds like the party was fun!"

As always, the boys offered her a hug as they entered the house. And she returned it in kind, patting their backs as she had when they were much younger.

"Your cookies were the first to go, Miss Ethel," Jayden said.

Jaxon offered his opinion. "That's because they're always better than anyone else's cookies."

"I agree!" Cael said, patting his stomach, giving evidence that he had eaten plenty.

"How would you know? You couldn't keep your eyes off of CarolAnn," Rafe laughed, wrapping his arms around an imaginary girl and swaying to the music coming from the radio.

"Yeah, well I didn't see the mistletoe that someone hung up. I noticed you didn't miss it. Not once," Cael retorted.

Zeke grinned. "Yeah, Rafe. How many different girls did you manage to get under the mistletoe?"

Puffing out his chest, Rafe quipped, "Too much goodness to go around for just one girl."

Zander rolled his eyes and moved into the living room, the other boys following.

"Well, how about I make some hot chocolate, or are you all completely full?" she asked. Glancing around at their wide-eyed expressions, a bubble of laughter erupted. "What a silly question! I've never known you boys to be completely filled up!"

"I'll help you, Miss Ethel," Cas said.

"Me, too," Asher added.

With their assistance, it didn't take long for Asher to carry in a large tray filled with mugs of hot chocolate and place it on the coffee table. Once she'd sat in her chair, the boys settled around... three on the sofa, two in the other chairs, and three on the floor, leaning back against the other furniture. The conversation was lively, continuing about who they saw, who they danced with, who was flirting. She could not help but smile as she listened to them reaffirming that they were, indeed, good young men. After a while, a calm silence ensued as they continued to sip their drinks.

Her quiet, contemplative Zander finally spoke. "This will be the last Christmas we'll all be together."

The air in her lungs stuttered to a halt, and she tried to steady her breath as she looked around at the shocked and anguished faces in front of her. *Oh, I've been so focused on my own grief as my children slowly move off into the world, but I forgot about their own fears.* With all eyes on her, she nodded slowly.

"Each of you is keenly aware of how life changes. Sometimes in the blink of an eye. Sometimes more slowly. Life doesn't stay the same, and nor do we. But I'll tell you what lasts, my dear boys. Love. And family. Each of you will go out into the world to find your own place, but always remember, your home here will always welcome you back."

Tears shone in their eyes, and she was glad she'd taught them to not be ashamed of their emotions. "Let's finish our celebration with a story. Zander, since you'll be away next year, you may choose."

It did not surprise her when he chose the same story to read that he had many years before... The Girl and the Winter Whirlwinds. And just as every time he told the tale, they all thought of how their ragtag family so resembled the characters all working together to save the spring.

The time had long since passed when she tucked the boys into bed at night, but she still managed to have a word with each one individually. She had started the habit with Zander, knowing that night was when his fears came out and she'd wanted to allay them. The habit became tradition, and the tradition became embedded in their very fiber.

Tonight, as they silently read in bed, she moved to Cas. "I saw you with Bianca earlier today in the yard. I know she's a lonely little girl, and it's very sweet of you to spend time with her." Bianca was a younger girl who had moved across the street with her father after her mother had died.

Shrugging, he said, "It's little enough that I can do for her. She's pretty cool." He smiled and added, "She likes my carvings."

"Then she has excellent taste," Ethel remarked. She bent, kissed his forehead, and whispered, "You were the last to come to me, and will be the last to leave. But never think for a moment that you are the last in my heart, my precious woodcarver." A slow smile spread across his face, and she patted his arm.

Standing, she looked at Zeke. His long hair was pulled back into a ponytail. She could not help but reach out and touch the thick tresses. He ducked his head slightly, and she smiled. "You were so afraid that your style would offend me. You forget that back in my day, many young men had long hair."

"Hippies, right?"

Laughter erupted as she nodded. "Yes, hippies."

He held his gaze and asked, "I can't imagine your George having long hair."

"Don't be so sure. While his hair would not have been long enough to pull back into a ponytail, it certainly dusted the bottom of his collar at one time." She thought back to the first time she saw him. "Ah, but he was a handsome man."

"Were you worried about him? When he joined the military?"

She remained silent, not wanting to offer a hasty reply. Instead, she asked one of her own. "Are you worried about Zander?"

His struggle was evident behind his eyes. His brow furrowed as he said, "Zander was the first to reach out to me. I was so… angry… all the time. I was angry about coming here. The other guys were bigger than me, but I was already thinking about how I could take them on." He snorted. "I would've so failed."

"Zander as well as the others became the big brothers you needed."

His head moved up and down slowly. "Yeah. I'm going to miss him. And I'm worried."

"And one day you will follow him."

His gaze jerked to hers and did not waver as they silently took measure of each other. "Yes."

She tried not to sigh, but her breath came out in a

76

rush. Nodding in little jerks, she said, "I told you that your name, Ezekiel, means strength. And Kemp means warrior or champion. You have always been a strong champion, my sweet Zeke. And wherever you go, whatever you do, you will protect."

She patted his leg, and with a whispered 'good night' moved to the other side of the room. Asher lounged in his bed, his long legs stretched out in front of him, his large book propped open. His gaze was intense as she approached. "You look like a young man with something on his mind."

"I was thinking about the Marines. I know Zander's going into the Army, and I've got years to decide, but…" his voice trailed off.

She sat on the edge of his bed and said, "Each of you came to me needing a sense of family. I've certainly made it no secret that I did as well. And I knew that there were things your older brothers could teach, help with, guide. But I hope I always gave you a sense of individuality. You are unique. And your choices will be unique, also."

Asher was not quick to smile, but when he did it always caused her heart to stutter with joy. And right now, while it was not a huge grin, his lips curved upward. "You always taught me that unique was not bad."

"Absolutely, unique is not a bad thing."

"I used to think it was just your nice way of saying that it was okay if I was ugly."

She swatted his leg, and he laughed. "Oh, you! You were never ugly. You looked into the mirror and saw what others had taunted. But you, my dear, sweet boy, are absolutely beautiful."

He blushed, and the tips of his ears turned bright red. "I'm not sure that beautiful is the right word to describe a future Marine, Miss Ethel."

"More's the pity," she quipped, her eyes twinkling. As their mirth settled, she added, "If the Marines are still calling to you when you're a senior, then you'll know the path to take. And whatever path that is, I'll be right here waiting for you to return."

His arms encircled her, and she felt him pat her back the way she always had his. "Good night, my dear."

She walked across the hall to the other large room, moving to Jaxon in his top bunk.

"I had something I wanted to ask you," he said, hesitation in his eyes, something she was not used to from him.

"Certainly. You can talk to me about anything."

"I've looked to see what the requirements are to be a volunteer for the rescue squad. I just didn't know how you'd feel about that since it's a volunteer position."

Cocking her head to the side, curiosity snaked through her. "Why do you think I'd have a problem with that?"

"Because it's volunteer... not paid. I know Zander, Cael, and Rafe have part-time jobs after school. But I really want to see what it would be like to be on the rescue squad. But I figure with my school load, I could squeeze in a part-time job along with being a volunteer."

"Jaxon, honey, I always wanted my boys to learn the

value of an honest job. But I never meant to imply that it had to be a paid position while you were still in high school. I would be thrilled for you to volunteer your time for something so worthwhile."

His shoulders heaved as he sighed in relief. "Really?"

Nodding, she prodded, "Tell me about it."

He sat up straighter, his eyes now bright with interest. "As part of their Junior Program, I can respond with them to emergency calls and learn to provide basic medical services. I'll become certified in CPR and then can take classes and training to be an EMT."

"Oh, my!" she exclaimed, surprised and yet pleased at what he'd be able to do. "Jaxon, I think that sounds amazing."

"Plus I've already looked, and I'd be able to do that after high school when I joined the military."

"I'm very impressed with how you've looked into this."

He grinned. "I'm not the only one. Jayden's been doing the same thing, too."

She glanced into the bottom bunk and saw Jayden listening closely to their conversation. "And what have you discovered?"

"I really want to be a mechanic," he said, his hesitation mirroring the earlier reaction from his twin. "I know you said we can go to college if we want to, but I really like working with my hands and tinkering with engines. The last time you took the van in to be worked on, I talked to the man who runs the shop. He said when I'm old enough, if I want a part-time job just helping out, I could have it."

"And is that something you'd like to do in the military as well?"

His lips curved into a smile. "Absolutely. Then I can get all the training and be paid at the same time!"

"Well, I think you two are planning your futures perfectly. I'm very proud of you."

"You always quoted from Roy Bennett. *'Don't just learn, experience'.*"

Laughing, she reached out with both hands and clutched theirs, giving a squeeze. "You're right. And remember... *'Don't just dream, do. Don't just exist, live.'*"

The bunk on the other side of the large room was empty, Rafe and Cael camping out in Zander's room talking. Even though the door was open, she knocked on the frame anyway, always careful with their privacy. The three young men looked up and smiled, and Rafe jumped up from the end of the bed, allowing her a chance to relax while he sat on the floor. "I don't want to interrupt," she said.

Cael snorted. "We were just telling Rafe that if he keeps working out the way he does, he could end up in a fitness magazine."

Rafe flexed his biceps, and she lifted her eyebrows. "Impressive, for sure. But then, Cael, you and Zander are just as muscular."

Zander rolled his eyes. "I don't think being in a magazine will ever be for me."

Cael gave a playful kick to Rafe while he sat on the floor and said, "Some of us plan on real work!"

"Hey, working on my body is real work!" Looking up at Miss Ethel, he added, "Speaking of real work, I was going to get some more straw mulch to put over the winter beds of roses. I can do that this weekend if that's okay."

"Oh, that would be lovely. Are you sure that instead of being a model you wouldn't rather be a gardener?"

Rafe shook his head. "I know that's what my dad did, but I don't think there's much money in it."

"There's more to life than money," Zander retorted.

"Yeah, but I discovered at the party tonight that the pretty girls drift toward either the guys who have money or the guys who have muscles. If I have both, I could have any pretty girl I want."

"There's nothing wrong with having good looks or money," Miss Ethel agreed. "But I think you'll find that looks are truly only skin deep. One day, you'll look beneath that." Glancing toward Cael, she asked, "Speaking of good looks, I thought you were very handsome at your sister's wedding."

He blushed and shook his head. "I don't think I ever want to get married, Miss Ethel."

Blinking in surprise, she tilted her head to the side, waiting for him to explain.

"It just seemed like a lot of trouble," he said, shrugging.

"It doesn't have to be. My George and I had a very simple wedding. He'd just gotten back from the Army, we had very little money and wanted to save it for getting a house. We had a little ceremony at the church and then my parents had a reception afterwards in their home."

Nodding, Zander said, "That makes sense. That's what I'll do. Well, if I ever get married."

"Oh, I think each of you will find your own princesses." She smiled at them, imagining the type of women that each of them would fall for.

Rafe stood and bent to kiss her cheek. "I don't need a princess, Miss Ethel, but I sure wouldn't mind somebody who cooked chicken the way you do."

Laughing, she patted his back as she hugged him and said good night.

Cael was next and he agreed. "Personally, I'd go for a woman that can make your cookies!"

The two boys stopped at the door, and Rafe looked over his shoulder. "It's not going to be the same without you, man." He glanced up at Cael and then back to Zander. "It was just the three of us for a while. The original brotherhood."

Swallowing past the lump in her throat, Ethel stayed quiet, allowing the moment of camaraderie and emotion to flow between her oldest boys as they stood on the precipice of manhood.

"Always brothers," Zander vowed. Cael and Rafe offered chin lifts and walked back to their room, leaving her and Zander alone.

Uncertain her voice would not shake, she remained quiet, noting he did the same. He swallowed deeply several times, and she had no doubt he worked to compose himself.

Finally, he said, "You gave me this."

She continued to wait quietly.

"You thought you were just giving me a safe place to

stay. But you gave me you. You gave me brothers. You gave me a family. You gave me life."

He shifted closer, and she wrapped her arms around him. It did not escape her notice that his grip was much stronger, and he was giving as much as he was taking. "For a while, it was just you and me, Zander. I want you to know that you were everything I could've ever wanted in a son." They pulled back, and she continued, "The next months will pass quickly. But always remember that this is your home. No matter where you go, no matter what you do, you can always come home. And I'll be waiting."

She leaned forward and kissed his cheek, wishing him a good night as she always did. Walking down the stairs, she began to turn off the lights. Moving into the living room, her hand was on the switch to flip off the Christmas tree lights when she saw George standing near the tree.

Tonight, she had no words, but the emotion flowed between them. He simply looked at her, smiled, and whispered into the dark, *"You did good. Merry Christmas, sweetheart."*

8

FIFTEEN YEARS LATER

Her house on Christmas Eve was filled to the brim with family. So much so that it was difficult to move between the living room, dining room, and kitchen. Laughter abounded. Kindhearted joking ensued. The patter of little feet as children raced around, calling out to each other, often made it difficult to hear what others were saying. But Ethel didn't mind. The house was far too quiet most of the time, so when family came to visit, especially all of the family at the same time, she would occasionally close her eyes and revel in the sounds of love.

Zander had found his sleeping beauty in Rosalie, a young woman that he had rescued, and who in turn had rescued him. Rafe had discovered true beauty in his wife, Eleanor, and the gardens he tended. Cael's match came in the form of a woman with long red hair who knew the meaning of sacrifice. Jaxon's mermaid, Morgan, had taught him the power of second chances. Jayden's petite wife, Ruby, gave true meaning to the words 'quiet perseverance'. Asher had been reunited with the girl he thought he'd lost in childhood, Penelope, his own beautiful swan. Zeke's wife, Cynthia, showed him that his strength combined with love was an unstoppable force. And Cas had been reunited with the little girl from across the street, now the beautiful woman, Bianca.

In between them all, twenty-one children of various ages filled the house. In warmer weather, they would spill out into the backyard where food-laden tables would hold their fare and picnic tables were placed under the shade of the large trees. But for the Christmas Eve meal, the women lined the counters with platters of food and the adults would squeeze around the table that Cas had enlarged over the years with new leaves. The children would sit amongst the adults or in their laps. No one seemed to mind the close quarters.

Ethel ate little, preferring to focus on the stories being told, the lives being shared, admiring the men that her boys had become, the women they had chosen as mates, and the children they were raising.

After the meal, she had little to do as the others made sure the dishes were washed and put away and the leftovers wrapped and placed into the refrigerator. They made their way into the living room where she sat in her favorite chair as the others filled every space. Gifts were shared based on the names they had drawn at Thanksgiving, and soon wrapping paper, bows, and ribbons lay in piles as everyone exclaimed over their presents.

"Nanny Ethel," the children cried. "Tell us a story!"

She thrilled them with stories of their dads as little boys. Continuing to create her tales, she wove in fairy-tales as she described how they met their princesses.

When it was time to say goodbye, the family made sure that the house was as clean as when they'd arrived. Fussing, she asked, "What will I do when you're gone?"

"You should rest, Miss Ethel," Zander said.

She waved off his words but knew that was exactly what she'd do. One by one, the families came over with hugs and kisses as they said goodbye. They all lived close, so she would see them in a few days, but she still held vigil on the porch and waved them goodbye as one by one they piled into their cars and drove off. A chilly wind swept past, sending her inside.

Standing in her foyer, the quiet closed in. Her gaze drifted up the stairway, the upstairs of the house only used when the grandchildren came to stay overnight.

As though pulled by a magnetic force, she held onto the banister and walked upstairs, standing in the hall, allowing the memories to flow. Her mind drifted to the many years that her boys slept safe and sound under her roof, their nightmares and loneliness chased away. For the first time in a long time, she cast her mind even further back to when one of the large bedrooms had been hers and George's. They had planned for the sound of children in the home, just not the way it happened.

But then, if she and George had had children of their own, she would've never had her boys.

Life is funny like that. You sometimes have to lose to

gain. You sometimes have to suffer to celebrate. You sometimes have to give up to be given.

Once again holding closely to the banister, she descended the staircase and moved into the kitchen. Fixing a cup of tea, she walked back down the hall. Passing the dining room, she glanced inside at the now quiet room. She remembered all the meals that she and George had shared sitting at one corner of the table, hoping that one day the table would be filled with family. And even though he was not with her, she had no doubt he would have been thrilled with the sight of everyone around, enjoying company and food. Sharing their lives. Sharing their love.

She made her way back into the living room and placed her teacup on the table before sitting in her favorite chair. She picked up her knitting and thought back over the day. But tonight, the clicking of the needles did not bring the same comfort that it always did, and she felt restless. Her eyes continually searched the room, waiting.

Finally, a touch on her shoulder startled her, and the air left her lungs in a rush as she looked up. "I was afraid you weren't coming," she confessed.

George squeezed her shoulder before walking over to the Christmas tree. *"My dear, Ethel, when have I ever missed Christmas?"*

They spent a few minutes in silence as he moved to the tree as he did each year, seeming to note the new ornaments placed by the children as well as the ones they had bought when first married.

"Did you see the boys earlier?" she asked.

He smiled. *"You should be so proud of them, sweetheart. They're all grown, healthy, happy. They've all found love. They are good men, good husbands, and wonderful fathers."*

She smiled, his reply moving through her, warming her deep inside. "I am proud, but I didn't do it alone. You were their father as much as I was their mother. I could not have done this... I could not have taken this journey if you had not been right beside me."

He walked over and knelt at her feet so his face was close to hers. She could swear she caught a scent of his aftershave and his eyes were just as deep. She lifted her hand to cup his face but halted, her fingers twitching, torn between wanting to touch him and knowing her hand would not encounter anything. "I love you, George."

She dropped her hand into her lap, allowing him to lean forward and brush a kiss against her lips instead. *"I love you, too, my sweet Ethel."*

He stood and started to move away, turning at the last moment, holding her gaze. *"Merry Christmas, sweetheart."*

As he slowly disappeared from view, she leaned back in her chair. The lights on the tree twinkled. The sound of carols floated throughout the room from her old radio. And the peace of the season settled over her. She lifted her eyes to the pictures on the bookshelves, illustrating a life well-lived. She particularly loved two with her and all the boys in frame next to the one of her and George's wedding. Smiling, she whispered into the dark, "Merry Christmas."

For all of Miss Ethel's boys:
Heroes at Heart (Military Romance)
Zander
Rafe
Cael
Jaxon
Jayden
Asher
Zeke
Cas

Please note that if you are a new-to-me reader, this companion novella is sweet, and my other books are written with scenes and language found in R-rated movies.
If you want to keep up with the latest Maryann Jordan news and fun giveaways and videos... join my Facebook reader group.
Maryann Jordan's Alpha Fan Group

Jaxon

Jayden

Asher

Zeke

Cas

Lighthouse Security Investigations

Mace

Rank

Walker

Drew

Blake

Tate

Hope City (romantic suspense series co-developed

with Kris Michaels

Brock book 1

Sean book 2

Carter book 3

Brody book 4

Kyle book 5

Ryker book 6

Rory book 7

Killian book 8

Saints Protection & Investigations

(an elite group, assigned to the cases no one else wants…or
can solve)

Serial Love

Healing Love

Revealing Love

Seeing Love

Honor Love

Sacrifice Love

Protecting Love

Remember Love

Discover Love

Surviving Love

Celebrating Love

Follow the exciting spin-off series:

Alvarez Security (military romantic suspense)

Gabe

Tony

Vinny

Jobe

SEALs

Thin Ice (Sleeper SEAL)

SEAL Together (Silver SEAL)

Letters From Home (military romance)

Class of Love

Freedom of Love

Bond of Love

The Love's Series (detectives)

Love's Taming

Love's Tempting

Love's Trusting

The Fairfield Series (small town detectives)

Emma's Home

Laurie's Time

Carol's Image

Fireworks Over Fairfield

Please take the time to leave a review of this book. Feel free to contact me, especially if you enjoyed my book. I love to hear from readers!

Facebook

Email

Website

ABOUT THE AUTHOR

I am an avid reader of romance novels, often joking that I cut my teeth on the historical romances. I have been reading and reviewing for years. In 2013, I finally gave into the characters in my head, screaming for their story to be told. From these musings, my first novel, Emma's Home, The Fairfield Series was born.

I was a high school counselor having worked in education for thirty years. I live in Virginia, having also lived in four states and two foreign countries. I have been married to a wonderfully patient man for thirty-five years. When writing, my dog or one of my four cats can generally be found in the same room if not on my lap.

Please take the time to leave a review of this book. Feel free to contact me, especially if you enjoyed my book. I love to hear from readers!

Facebook
Email
Website

Made in the USA
Coppell, TX
17 January 2021

48337059R00062